Ivy
the Worry
Fairy

by Daisy Meadows

ORCHARD

www.rainbowmagicbooks.co.uk

Ivy
the Worry
Fairy

Join the **Rainbow Magic Reading Challenge!**

Read the story and collect your fairy points to climb the Reading Rainbow at the back of the book.

This book is worth 10 points.

For Eleri and Megan, with love

Special thanks to
Rachel Elliot

ORCHARD BOOKS

First published in Great Britain in 2019 by The Watts Publishing Group

1 3 5 7 9 10 8 6 4 2

© 2019 Rainbow Magic Limited.
© 2019 HIT Entertainment Limited.
Illustrations © Orchard Books 2019

A CIP catalogue record for this book is available from the British Library.

ISBN 978 1 40835 510 7

Printed and bound in Great Britain by Clays Ltd, Elcograf S.p.A

MIX
Paper from
responsible sources
FSC® C104740

The paper and board used in this book are made from wood from responsible sources

Orchard Books
An imprint of Hachette Children's Group
Part of The Watts Publishing Group Limited
Carmelite House, 50 Victoria Embankment, London EC4Y 0DZ

An Hachette UK Company
www.hachette.co.uk
www.hachettechildrens.co.uk

Contents

Story One:
The Worry Stone

Story Two:
The Sparkling Spinner

Story Three:
The Serenity Balls

Jack Frost's Spell

Feeling worried, scared and small?
GREAT! That sounds like fun for all.
With Ivy's objects I will see
All humans steeped in misery.

Happy people aren't appealing.
I don't care how glad they're feeling!
Make them anxious – make them sad.
It feels so good to be this bad!

Story One
The Worry Stone

Chapter One
Sunrise at Olive House

"I can't believe we're both here," said
Rachel Walker.

"Me neither," said her best friend,
Kirsty Tate. "It was the best surprise ever
when we arrived last night and saw
you."

It was Saturday morning, and the

girls were looking forward to a relaxing weekend at the Olive House Family Mindfulness Retreat.

"Our parents are pretty good at keeping secrets," said Rachel, laughing. "They planned for us to be here together, and they didn't say a word about it."

The girls shared a very special secret of their own. Ever since they had first met, they had been friends with the fairies. They had been to Fairyland many times, and were always ready to help the fairies foil bad-tempered Jack Frost and his naughty goblins.

"We even get to share a bedroom," said Kirsty.

She sat on her bed and bounced up and down. The room was pretty, with sunshine-yellow curtains and a vase

of daffodils on the dressing table. The window looked out over the big garden of Olive House.

There was a knock on the door, and Rachel's mum came in with Kirsty's mum.

"Your dads have gone for an early

walk and we're going to join the
morning meditation class," said Mrs
Walker. "Would you like to come?"

"Yes please," said Kirsty, jumping to
her feet. "I want to try everything this
weekend."

"Me too," said Rachel. "Josh made

meditation sound amazing."

Josh was the Mindfulness Guide at
Olive House. The girls had met him
when they arrived the evening before.

"I thought so too," said Mrs Tate.
"I hope I can be as
calm and relaxed as
Josh by the end of this
weekend."

The meditation class
was being held in the
summerhouse in the
garden. It was a sunny
morning and birds
were singing loudly in
the leafy trees. When
Rachel and Kirsty
reached the summerhouse, they stopped
in surprise. Josh was there, but he didn't

look calm. His forehead was wrinkled
with worry lines.

"Good morning, Josh," said Mrs Walker.
"I'm afraid it's not a very good

morning so far," said Josh. "The chef is feeling too worried to cook breakfast, and there's something upsetting the yoga teacher, but we can't work out what's wrong. Everyone is anxious."

"It sounds as if everyone needs your meditation session this morning," said Mrs Tate.

But Josh shook his head.

"I'm feeling too worried to concentrate on meditating," he said. "I'm going to have to cancel this morning's class. I'm sorry."

He dashed back towards the house.

"Well, I wasn't

expecting a meditation expert to be so tense," said Mrs Walker. "Let's go and have some breakfast."

Kirsty and Rachel followed their mothers back to the house. In the dining hall, some of the other guests were chatting. They sounded upset.

"I'm so nervous," one woman was saying. "I feel sure that something is about to go wrong."

"I think that something has gone wrong already," said an older man, biting his nails. "They're just too scared to tell us about it."

Kirsty and Rachel looked around at the grown-ups and children nibbling at their breakfast. The morning sun was streaming through the windows. There were brightly coloured flowers in jam jars on every table. But no one looked very happy. The girls chose some cereal and juice, and sat down at a spare table.

"Olive House is supposed to help everyone feel calm and balanced inside," said Kirsty in between mouthfuls. "It felt like that last night when we arrived. But now I can't see a single smiling face."

"I hope people aren't going to feel like this all weekend," said Rachel. Suddenly, Kirsty noticed that the primroses on the table were glowing.

"Rachel, look," she whispered. "I think it's magic!"

Chapter Two
Ivy Appears

Rachel and Kirsty exchanged an excited glance. There was a booklet about the retreat on the table, and Kirsty quickly stood it up to hide the flowers from view. Then the primroses parted to reveal a tiny fairy.

"Hi, Rachel and Kirsty," she said,

fluttering out. "I'm Ivy the Worry Fairy."

The girls ducked down behind the booklet and smiled at her. She was wearing a pair of denim dungarees and a pink jacket, and her blonde hair was held back with a pink headband.

"Welcome to Olive House," said

Rachel. "We didn't expect to meet a fairy friend here today."

"I love coming to Olive House," said Ivy. "It's a wonderful retreat. I'm here quite often because of my fairy job."

"What is your job?" asked Kirsty.

Ivy's smile lit up her face.

"I help people manage their worries," she said. "Everyone feels worried from time to time, and it's important they know how to deal with it. I make sure that they don't let worrying stop them from enjoying life."

"I bet that's not always easy," said Rachel.

"You're right," said Ivy. "But I love helping people to feel better. And my three magical objects give me the special power to do that. But Jack Frost has stolen them."

"Oh no!" Kirsty exclaimed. "What are your magical objects?"

"My worry stone carries the magic

of awareness," Ivy explained. "It helps people understand why they are worried. The sparkling spinner helps people to stay active, distracting them from worries, and the serenity balls help people to stay positive."

"Why did Jack Frost take them?" Rachel asked.

Ivy sighed and sat down.

"I don't know," she said. "But without them, people everywhere are going to become more and more worried."

"That's what's been happening this morning,"

said Kirsty. "Everyone is anxious."

"What are they anxious about?" Ivy asked.

"No one seems to know," Rachel replied. "They're just ... worrying."

"It's because my worry stone is missing," said Ivy. "If a person knows why they're worried, it's easier to cope. But without the stone, no one will understand their own feelings."

"Then the worry stone has to be found," said Kirsty in a determined voice. "We'll help."

"Jack Frost gave the worry stone to a goblin, and I followed him here," said Ivy. "Will you let me turn you into fairies so we can search for him?"

The girls nodded. "Let's not waste a moment," said Rachel. "We have to

find a place where you can turn us into
fairies without being seen."

Chapter Three
A Strange Yoga Student

Rachel held open her dress pocket, and Ivy darted inside. Then the girls slipped out of the dining hall and looked around.

"How about in there?" asked Kirsty, pointing to the cupboard under the stairs.

Giggling, she and Rachel scrambled inside the little cupboard. They bumped

into mops, brooms and buckets in the
half-darkness.

"Now," said Ivy.

She popped out of Rachel's pocket and
waved her wand. Sparkling flecks of fairy
dust whisked the girls into the air and
twirled them around.

"Turning into a fairy is such a lovely feeling," said Kirsty.

Gauzy wings fluttered on their backs and they shrank to fairy size. Rachel and Kirsty shared a smile.

"Let's go and find that goblin," said Rachel.

She swooped out through the keyhole, and Kirsty and Ivy followed her. To their

33

alarm, there was a crowd of people in the hallway.

"This way to the yoga class," Josh was saying.

The fairies zoomed up to the high ceiling.

"My heart's going pitter-patter," said Kirsty. "Do you think anyone saw us?"

"I think someone did," said Rachel
suddenly.

She pointed to the entrance, where a
green leg was just disappearing around
the door.

"The goblin," Ivy cried. "Follow him!"

Outside Olive House, the goblin was
leapfrogging over the croquet hoops.

"He's going to be seen," said Kirsty,
groaning.

"He knows, but he doesn't care," said
Ivy. "He's got the worry stone."

The goblin tripped over a croquet hoop
and landed on his back, giggling. Then
he saw the fairies staring down at him.

"Fairies!" he yelled, pointing a knobbly
finger at them. "I've got your silly stone –
and you can't have it back!"

"Oh no," said Rachel as the goblin jumped up and ran off. "He's heading towards the yoga class."

There was a large group of people standing next to the summerhouse, including Mrs Walker and Mrs Tate. Josh was at the front beside a young woman. She was wearing a plain black tank top and black yoga pants, and her long hair was tied back.

"This is Christy," Josh said. "She'll be teaching you some simple yoga today."

The fairies flew to a leafy tree and perched on a branch.

"Josh looks worried," said Kirsty.

"So does Christy," Rachel added.

The people in the class looked worried too.

"No one else will be able to enjoy this class unless I get my worry stone back," Ivy said.

"Look, there's the goblin," said Kirsty.

The goblin elbowed his way to the front of the group. He was wearing a neon yellow yoga outfit and a yellow

cap pulled low
over his face.
Christy put her
palms together
and bowed to the
class. Cackling
with laughter,
the goblin sat
down and started
to twist his legs
around his neck. Everyone stared at him.

"It's great that you're so keen," said
Christy, smiling at the goblin. "But let's
start with something simple. Focus on
your body, breathe in, and copy me."

The goblin copied her, and so did Mrs
Walker and Mrs Tate. The others just
shuffled their feet.

"They're too worried to try," said Ivy.

Christy gazed around at her class, looking upset.

"I bet the goblin's hiding the worry stone under his cap," said Kirsty. "He doesn't have a bag or any pockets."

"But we can't fly up to his cap," said Ivy. "Everyone would see us. What are we going to do?"

Chapter Four
Undercover!

Suddenly, an idea popped into Kirsty's head.

"Ivy, can you turn us into butterflies?" she asked. "No one would be surprised to see butterflies."

"That's a great idea," said Ivy, raising her wand.

"Colours of the earth and sky,
Camouflage us while we fly!"

The leaves above the fairies began to
shiver, sprinkling the fairies with coloured
dust. As it touched them, their wings
changed shape. Their fairy bodies grew
long and fluffy, with antennae and big,
dark eyes.

"Kirsty, your wings are so beautiful," said Rachel.

Kirsty had turquoise wings with a pattern of white and yellow swirls. Rachel's wings were orange with tiny black circles, and Ivy had become deep red with yellow and black stripes.

"Come on," said Kirsty. "Let's get that stone back!"

The butterfly-fairies flapped their way towards the goblin.

"It's hard to fly with different wings," said Rachel, panting.

A few people glanced at them as they flew past, but they looked away again.

"They're too busy feeling worried to notice butterflies," said Kirsty. "I feel sorry for them."

"The best way to help them is to get

the worry stone back," said Ivy.

The three butterflies landed on the goblin's cap. They were so light that he didn't feel a thing. He went on stretching and bending.

"I see a way in at the back of the cap," said Kirsty.

Laying their wings flat, they slipped inside the cap. It was hard to see at first, but then their eyes got used to the darkness.

"I think I can see the worry stone," Rachel whispered.

She started to crawl up the goblin's bony head. In the darkness, something was glowing softly.

"I see it too," said Ivy.

They all crawled towards the glow. Then the goblin giggled.

"What's that tickling my head?" he said.

"Oh no," said Kirsty. "We forgot how many tiny, tickly feet we have now that we're butterflies. Hold on tight!"

They clung to his head as he jiggled around. There were shouts of surprise from the people around him. Then the three butterfly-fairies started bumping up and down as if they were on a trampoline.

"He's running," cried Kirsty.

With a wave of Ivy's wand, they were all fairies again.

"Hold on to his hair," she shouted. "Don't let go!"

"YOWCH!" he yelled as they clutched at his hair. "Get off!"

He tore the cap off and flung it to the ground, fairies and all. They landed with a bump behind a large bush, and the worry stone flew into the air and out of sight.

"Oh no!" cried Ivy.

"At least we're safe," Rachel panted. "I thought we were going to be seen."

"I can see you!" yelled the goblin, his hands on his hips. "Was that you tickling my head?"

"Yes," said Rachel, scrambling out of the cap. "We were trying to get Ivy's worry stone back. I'm sorry we scared you."

"Apology not accepted," the goblin

snapped. "Besides, I wasn't scared."

"Where is the stone?" wondered Kirsty. The fairies spun around, scanning the grass. Then they saw something glowing in a clump of primroses.

"That's it!" cried Ivy.

Chapter Five
Worry Stone Rescue

Rachel dived towards the worry stone, but the goblin pounced and snatched it up. He squawked with laughter.

"That doesn't belong to you," said Kirsty. "As long as you have it, people will feel anxious without knowing why.

Please give it back. It's the right thing to do."

"I don't care," said the goblin. He sat down and stuck out his bottom lip.

"We can't let you keep it," said Rachel gently. "We won't stop trying until we get it back."

"Jack Frost says you're a pack of pests," said the goblin.

"Why does he want Ivy's magical objects anyway?" Kirsty asked.

The goblin sniggered.

"Jack Frost is going to stop all your boring positive thinking and happiness," he said. "He wants to have some fun with ice and misery."

"But you were enjoying yourself in the yoga class," said Kirsty, perching on the goblin's knee. "That's the kind of thing that Jack Frost will spoil if he has the worry stone. Besides, he's not going to let you keep it, is he?"

The goblin frowned, and then his shoulders drooped.

"I'm worried about getting into trouble with Jack Frost," he said in a small voice.

Ivy smiled at him. "That's because my worry stone is in the wrong hands. Once I get it back, you won't be afraid of Jack

Frost any more. You'll remember that you are strong, and you won't let him bully you!"

That decided it. The goblin stood up and held his head high.

"You're right!" he cried. "I'm a tough goblin, and no one scares me!"

He tossed the worry stone into the grass and tottered off towards the summerhouse, shaking his fists in the air.

With a cry of happiness, Ivy put her arms around the stone. It instantly shrank to fairy size.

"Thank you from the bottom of my heart," she said to Rachel and Kirsty. "You have taken one of my worries away."

She flicked her wand, and Rachel and Kirsty felt themselves spinning around,

growing bigger and bigger until they were human-sized again.

"I'm going to take my worry stone back home," said Ivy. "Thank you both so much."

"You're welcome," said Rachel, smiling.

"Make sure you come back soon," Kirsty added. "We want to help you find your other magical objects too."

Ivy disappeared in a puff of golden fairy dust. Rachel and Kirsty shared a hug.

"I do hope we can find the other objects," said Rachel. "It's awful seeing everybody so worried."

"We will," said Kirsty, taking her best friend's hand. "And as long as we're together, we've got nothing to worry about. We've got each other!"

Story Two
The Sparkling Spinner

Chapter Six
A Lazy Day

The next morning, Kirsty and Rachel were reading the Olive House timetable while they ate breakfast with their parents.

"It's so hard to decide what to try next," said Rachel. "Everything sounds like lots of fun, and all the things we did yesterday were amazing."

The girls shared a secret smile.

"It felt good to help Ivy," said Kirsty in a quiet voice. "I loved seeing how everyone relaxed after we found the worry stone."

"We've tried yoga, meditation and breathing exercises," said Rachel, ticking them off on her fingers. "What's next?"

"How about some organic gardening?" said Mr Walker. "Your mums are going to try massage therapy, but I want to work outside today."

"Gardening sounds like fun," said Kirsty.

"I'll join you," said Mr Tate. "I love digging and making things grow."

They finished breakfast and went to find the organic garden. A young woman was digging in the vegetable patch. She rested her foot on her spade and smiled at them.

"Hi," she said, pushing blonde hair out of her eyes. "I'm Connie, and I'm the Olive House gardener."

More people joined them, and Connie asked them to stand in a circle.

"Welcome to the organic garden," she said. "Here, we do useful work. We grow the food we eat and chop up the wood for the fire. While we work, we can let our worries go. It's what we call mindful gardening. We are aware of our worries, and being aware helps us let go of them."

Connie showed them around the little garden, telling them about all the different jobs that needed to be done. Everyone chose something to do. Mr Tate and Mr Walker picked up two axes.

"We'll chop wood," said Mr Walker.

"Shall we pick the lettuce?" Rachel asked. "It all looks so green and fresh."

The girls got down on their hands and knees and started to cut the lettuce.

"Remember, everyone," said Connie, "during mindful gardening we think only about the work."

The girls worked quietly, thinking about the shape and feel of the plants they were cutting. They didn't notice the time pass by. They didn't think about what anyone else was doing. But when they finished the row and looked up, all the others had disappeared.

"That's odd," said Rachel. "Where is everyone?"

"It's very quiet," said Kirsty. "I can't hear any sounds of digging or chopping."

They walked around the side of the garden shed and then stopped in surprise. Connie and the rest of the gardening

group were sitting on the ground, staring down at the grass.

"We've finished the lettuce," said Rachel.

Connie glanced up and gave her a half-smile.

"That's nice," she said.

"What would you like us to do next?" Kirsty asked.

Connie shrugged.

"It doesn't matter," she said. "Why not sit down and have a rest?"

"But what about mindful gardening?" asked Rachel. "What about connecting with nature?"

"Maybe tomorrow," said Connie. "I'm worrying about how to stop slugs eating all the plants."

Kirsty went over to her dad.

"Did you chop up all the wood?" she asked.

"We got tired," said Mr Tate. "And a bit stressed. I keep thinking about work. I've got lots to do in the office next week."

"But you're not supposed to be thinking about your job," said Kirsty. "It's the weekend."

"I've got so much DIY to do around the house," said Mr Walker, frowning. "I can't stop worrying about it."

"But you came here to get rid of worries," said Rachel.

Mr Walker just shook his head and rested his head in his hands.

"This must be because two of Ivy's magical objects are still missing," said Kirsty in a quiet voice.

"Let's go and work on the garden some more," said Rachel. "I feel that if I sit down, I'll start thinking about my worries too."

They walked down to the bottom of the garden together and started to do some weeding of the flowerbeds. But they had hardly started when Kirsty gave a cry of surprise.

"Look at that weed," she said. "It's glowing."

Rachel pulled on the weed, and it came easily out of the ground. Ivy the Worry Fairy was clinging to the roots!

Chapter Seven
Goblin Gardeners

"Good morning," said Ivy. "Are you enjoying gardening?"

"We were," said Kirsty. "But no one else is joining in. Even the teacher is just sitting down and worrying."

"They've lost their energy because my sparkling spinner is missing," Ivy said. "It helps keep people active. Without it, they are too preoccupied with their worries to do anything else."

"Does that mean that people will be tired and worried until we find the sparkling spinner?" Rachel asked.

Ivy nodded.

"But I might have good news," she said. "I came to tell you that there are two goblins down by the meditation lake. I saw one of them holding something silvery, and I think it's my sparkling spinner. But I didn't dare to get too close on my own. Will you help me?"

"Of course we will," said Kirsty at once. "Let's go down to the meditation lake right now."

Ivy slipped under Kirsty's hair and the girls ran across the lawn towards the lake. As they ran, they saw a few other people from the retreat.

"Everyone looks really sad and low on energy," said Rachel, slowing down.

They reached the winding path that led to the lake and jogged along it. The path grew narrower and more brambly.

"This is all very worrying," Kirsty said, stopping beside a bush. "Will we ever get the sparkling spinner back? Is the path too narrow and dangerous? What will happen if we fail?"

Rachel sat down on the path beside her.

"You're right," she said. "I suddenly feel so tired."

Ivy fluttered out from underneath Kirsty's hair.

"Everyone at Olive House is worn out from thinking about their troubles," she said. "I can't let the same thing happen to you. I have an idea."

She closed her eyes and waved her wand.

"Now that my worry stone is safely back in Fairyland, I can use a little of its magic," she said.

"Worry stone, I need you here.
Your mindful-magic task is clear.
Stay beside my friends today.
Keep their worried thoughts at bay."

A wisp of fairy dust looped around the girls and then disappeared.

"Oh, I suddenly feel all fizzy with energy," said Kirsty.

"My head feels clear and calm!" added Rachel.

"We all need to keep active and use our energy in a good way," said Ivy. "My spell won't last for ever, but it will give you a bit of help."

"Thanks," said Rachel, standing up. "I feel ready to face the goblins now."

They hurried along the overgrown path. Before they reached the sparkling lake, they heard loud squawks of laughter on the path ahead.

"That sounds like goblins," said Rachel.

The girls crept further along until they reached a curve in the path. Just around the bend, there was a little clearing. The goblins were kneeling down beside a patch of wild violets.

"Are they gardening?" asked Kirsty in surprise. "Has the sparkling spinner made them want to do something kind?"

Rachel took a closer look and shook her head.

"No," she said. "They're pulling up all the beautiful plants and leaving the weeds to grow."

"We have to stop them before they spoil this place for everyone else," said Kirsty. "But how?"

Chapter Eight
Endless Energy

The goblins cackled with laughter as they tore plant after plant out of the ground. Violets, daffodils, crocuses and tulips were flung over their shoulders.

"Why are they doing this?" Rachel asked.

"The sparkling spinner has given them

lots of distracting energy," whispered Ivy. "They're busy doing things that distract them from their worries."

"Gardening is fun," said the first goblin, who had a large green bow stuck to his head. He threw more flowers into the air.

"Gardening goblin style is fun," said the smaller goblin, picking his nose.

"Oh dear," said Ivy. "The sparkling spinner is giving them bags of energy. They will spend all day doing things that distract them from their worries."

"You've given me an idea," said Kirsty suddenly. "When people have lots of energy, and do what they love they also feel happy and healthy. Let's play with them and have some fun. When they see that we want to be friendly, they might feel cheerful enough to want to give us the sparkling spinner back."

"I like that idea," said Rachel. "I hope it works."

"Let's start with a dance," said Ivy.

She swished her wand, and the air was filled with loud, fast music. Rachel exchanged a nervous smile with Kirsty.

"I'm not a brilliant dancer," she said.

"That doesn't matter – knowing the right steps and making the right shapes aren't important," said Ivy.

"Dancing is all about having fun."

The goblins were looking around in amazement.

"Where's that music coming from?" asked the goblin with the bow.

Just then, Rachel and Kirsty sprang out from behind a bush. They leapt and

swayed to the music. Rachel tried to remember everything she had learned in her ballet class. Kirsty waved to the goblins.

"Come and dance with us," she called

out in a friendly way.

At first, the goblins shook their heads. But as the girls twirled around, the goblins started to tap their feet. The music got faster, and at last the goblin with the bow jumped up.

"Yeah, I am the best dancer in the world!" he exclaimed, twisting his hips and flapping

his elbows like wings.
"I've got the coolest
moves."

"You look stupid,"
yelled the other goblin,
also jumping up.
"Watch me. I should
win prizes for my
dancing. People should
give me medals."

He stuck out his
bottom and waggled it
around.

"Boogie boogie," he sang, completely
out of time with the music. "Boogie
boogie."

Everyone giggled and copied the
goblin's dance moves. Rachel and Kirsty
were soon out of breath from all the

whirling, twirling and laughing.

"Please can we do something else now?" said Rachel after she had been spinning around for fifteen minutes. "I'm getting dizzy."

"OK," said Kirsty. "How about making some music?"

Ivy waved her wand again, and a large box appeared in front of the goblins. It was filled with all sorts of musical instruments. The goblin with the bow chose a drum, and the other goblin grabbed a recorder. Rachel picked out a triangle and Kirsty took a pair of

maracas. Ivy stayed out of sight behind a bush.

"I'll be the leader," said Rachel. "Everyone follow me and play as loud as you can."

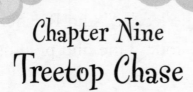

Chapter Nine
Treetop Chase

Rachel skipped around the little clearing, pinging her triangle. She jumped over boulders and balanced on tree stumps. The goblins copied her every move. The recorder tooted and the drum banged. Kirsty was at the back, shaking her maracas.

"This is fun!" shouted one of the goblins.

After ten minutes, Rachel and Kirsty were puffing and panting, but the goblins were still full of energy.

"I'm completely out of breath," said Kirsty, dropping down beside a patch of squashed violets.

"Weedy little human," the second goblin scoffed.

"I'm bored of playing instruments," said the goblin with the bow.

He threw the drum down. It vanished as it hit the ground.

"What shall we do now?" he demanded, glaring at the girls. "Think of something for us to play."

"Of course," said Rachel. "Goblins love

games. How about football?"

Behind the bush, Ivy waved her wand. Suddenly, the goblins and the girls were wearing football kit. A whistle blew, and Rachel saw a ball at her feet.

"Let's try to get these goblins smiling," she whispered to Kirsty.

The girls and the goblins ran, kicked, dived and defended. They lost three balls in the woods. For a while, the goblins laughed and had fun. But then they started to squabble about the rules. Rachel and Kirsty stumbled over to the bush where Ivy was hiding.

"It's no good," said Kirsty. "They don't want to be friends."

"Maybe we should be honest with them," said Rachel. "Let's ask them to give back the sparkling spinner. Maybe they'll surprise us."

Ivy waved her wand and the girls were back in their own clothes. They walked towards the goblins, who were squabbling over the football. Ivy flew along beside them.

"Excuse me," Rachel said. "I think

you have something that belongs to our friend."

"Go away and leave us alone," snapped the goblin with the bow. "We're busy."

"Please give the sparkling spinner back," said Kirsty.

"You can't tell us what to do," the smaller goblin shouted.

Both goblins blew raspberries and then turned and ran.

"Come back!" cried Rachel.

The girls and Ivy raced after them. Squealing, the goblins scrambled into a tree. They clambered up the branches as fast as they could.

"I've got a splinter," wailed the goblin with the bow.

"I think I'm allergic to trees," squawked the smaller one.

Rachel and Kirsty pulled themselves up too.

"Stop," Rachel called.

She tried to catch the goblin with the bow by his ankle. He kicked his legs and swung higher. Then he pulled something small and silver from under his bow.

"My sparkling spinner!" exclaimed Ivy.

Ivy's sudden shout shocked the goblin. His hand jerked, and the sparkling spinner slipped through his fingers.

"No!' he yelled.

Chapter Ten
Lost and Found

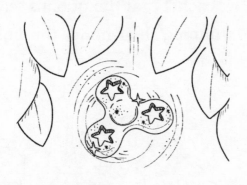

Everyone stared as the sparkling spinner bounced off branches and disappeared through the leaves. There was a faint thump as it landed somewhere below. For a moment, they all stared at each other. Then Ivy swooped towards the ground, while the girls and the goblins dropped back through the branches as fast as they could.

"Where did it land?" asked Kirsty as she bumped to the ground.

Ivy was zigzagging among the blades of grass. Rachel and the goblins scrabbled around, running their hands through the grass.

"Find it," screeched the smaller goblin.

Kirsty tripped over a stone and fell against the tree. Something small and silver was lying between two roots. Kirsty's heart started beating like a drum.

"I've found it," she exclaimed.

The sparkling spinner glittered as she held it up. Ivy zoomed towards it, and it shrank to fairy size as soon as she touched it.

"Thank goodness," said Rachel.

The goblins threw themselves to the ground, groaning and wailing.

"You meanies!" shouted the one with the bow. "Now we're going to be in Jack Frost's bad books, and it's all your fault."

"I don't want anyone to be in Jack Frost's bad books," said Ivy in a gentle voice.

She waved her wand, and suddenly the goblins' arms were filled with sprays of tiny blue flowers. The heart-shaped petals looked as if they had been sprinkled with silver.

"This plant is called 'Jack Frost'," Ivy told the goblins. "It likes darker, shady places, so it should be happy at the Ice Castle. You can give it to him as a present. I hope it stops him from being cross with you."

The goblins looked at each other, and their grumpy frowns melted away.

"We're going to be the most popular goblins ever!" squawked the one with the bow. "Hurray!"

Ivy waved her wand again, and the goblins disappeared.

"I've sent them back to Fairyland," she said. "I should go too, and put the sparkling spinner back where it belongs. Thank you, Rachel and Kirsty. I don't know what I would do without you."

"We're so happy you found your sparkling spinner," said Kirsty.

Ivy smiled. Then there was a flurry of

fairy dust, and she had gone.

"Race you back to the organic
garden," said Rachel.

Laughing, the best friends ran back
along the brambly path and across the
lawn. The organic garden was filled with
smiling, enthusiastic people. Connie was

planting seeds, and the girls could see Mr Tate and Mr Walker chopping wood.

"Now the sparkling spinner is back where it belongs, Olive House is going to be more fun than ever," said Kirsty. "We only have one of Ivy's magical objects left to find."

"I wonder where Jack Frost has hidden the serenity balls," said Rachel.

"I'm sure Ivy will come and find us as soon as she has a clue," said Kirsty. "But right now, we've got some gardening to do!"

Story Three
The Serenity Balls

Chapter Eleven
The Olive Workshop

It was Sunday evening, and the girls and their parents were standing in the entrance hall of Olive House.

"This has been a lovely weekend," said Mrs Tate with a happy sigh.

"I can't decide what I enjoyed the most," said Rachel.

"Gardening was my favourite," said Kirsty, adding in a whisper, "after we got Ivy's sparkling spinner back where it belongs."

"There's one more thing to enjoy," said Mrs Walker, looking at her programme. "It's a feelings workshop for everyone."

"That sounds interesting," said Mr Walker. "I'm starting to really enjoy sharing my feelings."

The girls followed their parents into the large sitting room. Everyone found a seat, and Rachel and Kirsty shared a squashy beanbag. Josh, Christy and Connie were next to the fireplace.

"Welcome to the final event of our time together," said Josh, the Mindfulness Guide. "This workshop is my favourite moment of the weekend. This is where

we hear how you are feeling, and what you think of your time here at Olive House."

"It's been a good weekend," said a tall lady in an irritable voice. "But I don't suppose it will help when I get back home. I'll still have the same old worries to think about."

"That's how I feel, too," said a man with a long, bushy beard. "This weekend has been fun, but I don't see how talking about my feelings will make a difference when I get home."

Lots of people were nodding, and Rachel remembered that Ivy's serenity balls could help people to think calm thoughts and talk about their feelings, even when they were sad or worried.

"We have to find the serenity balls before the end of the weekend," she whispered into Kirsty's ear. "If we don't, no one will leave feeling good."

Kirsty squeezed her hand.

"We can do it," she said.

Christy stepped forward and opened her mouth to speak. Then she stopped. She didn't move a muscle. Rachel and Kirsty looked at their parents. They were also standing completely still, like statues.

"They've been frozen," said Rachel.

She jumped up and waved her hand in front of her mother's face. Mrs Walker didn't blink.

"Look at the fire," said Kirsty.

The flames were frozen too. They had stopped as they flickered upwards.

"Oh my goodness, is this Jack Frost's

work?" asked Kirsty.

"No," said a familiar voice. "It's my work."

The girls looked up and saw Ivy sitting on the mantelpiece and swinging her legs.

"Don't worry," she said. "The queen lent me a special spell so that I could pause time, come in here and whisk you both away without anyone seeing a thing. You see, I've found out where the serenity balls are."

"That's wonderful," Rachel said. "Are you sure the people here won't remember anything?"

"You will come back to the exact

moment you left," Ivy promised. "They won't even have blinked."

Rachel and Kirsty held hands as the little fairy raised her wand. Orange and red sparkles danced around them.

"This magic is tickly," Kirsty giggled.

A moment later they had shrunk to fairy size, and their gauzy wings were lifting them into the air.

"We must hurry," said Ivy. "Time may be standing still here, but in Fairyland Jack Frost hasn't stopped causing trouble."

She fluttered over to a candlestick that stood on the end of the mantelpiece. At a tap of her wand, it moved sideways. There was a hole underneath, with a long slide going down.

"Where does it go?" said Rachel.

"All the way to Fairyland," said Ivy with a smile. "Follow me!"

Chapter Twelve
Soft Landing

The fairies whizzed down the slide, feeling as if they must be speeding towards the centre of the earth. But at last they shot out into the sunshine and landed on something soft, white and puffy.

"Where are we?" asked Rachel, trying

to catch her breath.

"We're on a cloud, high above Fairyland," said Ivy. "I thought that this was a good way to reach Jack Frost without being seen. The Woodland Fairies told me that they had spotted him in a meadow near here."

"It's a very comfortable way to travel!" said Kirsty, bouncing up and down on the white fluff.

The fairies lay on their tummies and peered over the edge of the cloud. They were floating above a meadow. Goblin guards were standing in a circle around Jack Frost, facing outwards. He was sitting with his legs crossed and his eyes shut. His hands were resting palm-up on his knees.

"Goodness, he looks as if he's

meditating," said Rachel in surprise.

"Can you see what's in his hands?" asked Ivy in an excited voice.

She flicked her wand and a pair of sparkling silver binoculars appeared in Rachel's hand. She put them to her eyes and looked down. In each hand, Jack Frost was holding a shining green ball.

He was steadily squeezing and releasing them.

"Are those the serenity balls?" Rachel asked. "They're beautiful." Ivy nodded, and Kirsty took the binoculars so that she could look too.

"The serenity balls help people to talk about their feelings, even when they are sad or worried," Ivy reminded the girls. "Talking about feelings is much healthier than bottling them up. It helps people to feel calmer. But as long as my serenity balls are down there, no one will be able to talk about how they feel – and they won't be able to let go of their worries."

"How are we going to get the serenity

balls back?" Kirsty asked. "Jack Frost has goblins all around him."

"We have to find a way to get closer," said Rachel.

"The goblins will spot us whether we fly or walk," Ivy remarked. "The only things in the meadow are grass, insects and flowers."

"Then that's exactly what we have to become," said Kirsty, jumping up on to her feet. "Ivy, can you make us look like daisies?"

"Good thinking, Kirsty," said Rachel. "The goblins will never see us."

A few moments later, three little daisies floated down to the meadow on the breeze. The goblins didn't notice the tiny flowers landing among the bright-green blades of grass. They didn't spot

the daisies weaving closer to them. They certainly didn't hear the daisies whispering to each other. All the goblins could hear were the words of Jack Frost, and they were feeling fed up.

"He's been talking for hours," grumbled a short goblin.

"I'm hungry," another goblin complained, dangling a daisy chain from his left ear.

The three fairies heard every word.

They slipped closer to Jack Frost and listened.

"It all started to go wrong when Jilly Chilly turned up," the Ice Lord was saying in a strangely calm, singsong voice. "She was the reason for a lot of my problems. She was so bossy and annoying. I hope she stays in the ice mountains

where I sent her. But maybe I would feel better if I told her how I feel. Yes, that's a very good idea. Goblins, we're going to the ice mountains to see my sister Jilly Chilly."

Chapter Thirteen
A Risky Plan

"Are you sure, my lord?" asked the short goblin in a tired voice. "Five minutes ago you told us that all your problems were caused by Frosty and the Gobolicious Band not being famous enough, and you wanted us to plan a concert for the whole of Fairyland."

"Don't question me!" Jack Frost screeched, and then he cleared his throat and his oddly calm voice returned. "Yes, I remember now. I want to be Frosty again. I want to give a concert so that I can tell everyone in Fairyland how I am feeling and become super famous. That is what I really need."

"It's not what I really need," groaned the goblin with the daisy chain.

The three fairy daisies huddled together.

"What's the matter with Jack Frost?" asked Kirsty.

"I think he's using the serenity balls to try to keep himself calm," said Ivy. "But their magic is powerful, and he isn't using them with care. They're making him exaggerate every little feeling he has."

"All I want is to stop humans from

working out their troubles," Jack Frost went on. "I like the misery and worry, as long as it happens to other people and not to me."

Rachel looked around and noticed that some of the goblins had their hands over their ears.

"I don't think that the magic is working on the goblins," she said. "Listening to Jack Frost's feelings doesn't seem to be making them feel calm."

"That gives me an idea," said Kirsty. "All the goblins are facing outwards, away from Jack Frost. They won't see us if we are inside the circle. They've got their hands over their ears – can

you use magic to make them not hear
anything at all? I bet they'd be glad if
we stopped them from hearing his voice.
We could become fairies again, creep up
behind Jack Frost and just lift the serenity
balls out of his open hands. The goblins
wouldn't hear him shouting for help and
that might just give us enough time to
get away."

Ivy's eyes opened very wide.

"Lift the serenity balls out of his
hands?" she repeated. "That sounds very
risky. What if he catches us?"

"It's a risk we have to take," said Kirsty
in a firm voice. "This is our best chance,
Ivy. We must try."

"You're right," said Ivy, biting her lip.
"Without the serenity balls, people will
forget about thinking calm thoughts or

talking about their feelings. Everyone will
be worried and irritable."

"Let's do it," said Rachel.

They slipped inside the ring of goblins
and Ivy waved her wand in a wide
circle. At once, a glowing ring of green
appeared around each goblin's head.
Then Rachel and Kirsty felt their white

petals fluttering, and they whooshed up
to the size of fairies again.

"I worry that I might never beat those
pesky fairies," Jack Frost was saying.
"They're tricky little cheats, and they're
always spoiling my most brilliant plans.
What if they manage to stop me this
time? How can I spread misery and
unhappiness while the Worry Fairy is
making everyone feel calm and focused?"

Kirsty signalled to Rachel that she
would take Jack Frost's left hand. Rachel
crept up on his right side.

Squeeze – release – squeeze – release: Jack
Frost's hands were clenching around the
serenity balls in a steady pattern. Rachel
and Kirsty exchanged a knowing glance.
They had to take the balls at exactly
the same moment. They knew that they

could trust their strong bond of friendship.
Squeeze – release – squeeze – release.

"One …" mouthed Kirsty silently, "…
two … three!"

Chapter Fourteen
Royal Help

At exactly the same moment, Rachel and Kirsty snatched the serenity balls out of Jack Frost's hands and darted backwards.

"Hey!" yelled Jack Frost.

The goblins didn't move, but Jack Frost lunged out and caught Rachel's wrist in an iron grip.

"Let me go!" she cried, twisting to get away from him.

With a loud crack of lightning, Rachel and Jack Frost completely disappeared.

"Rachel!" cried Kirsty, turning to Ivy in alarm. "We have to save her!"

"But I don't know where he's gone," Ivy exclaimed. "He could be anywhere."

"The Seeing Pool could tell us," said Kirsty. "Can you magic us all to the

Fairyland Palace?"

For answer, Ivy flicked her wand and a puff of sparkles burst around them. Kirsty blinked and saw that they were standing on the steps of the palace. Its pink turrets were glowing in the sunshine, and flags fluttered from every spire.

"Come on," said Kirsty.

She ran up the steps and knocked on the door. It opened at once. Bertram the frog footman smiled at her.

"Please, may I see the queen?" Kirsty said in a breathless voice.

"Her Majesty is always happy to see friends of Fairyland," said Bertram with a little bow.

Kirsty zoomed down the gleaming corridor to the throne room. She stopped so suddenly in the doorway that Ivy bumped into her back. Queen Titania was busy reading an important-looking scroll of paper. She looked up and the fairies curtsied.

"Kirsty, welcome to Fairyland," said the queen. "Thank you for helping Ivy. Have you found the serenity balls?"

"We have one of them, Your Majesty," said Kirsty. "But something terrible has happened. Jack Frost has kidnapped Rachel and we don't know where they are."

Instantly, they were standing beside the Seeing Pool in the palace garden. Kirsty felt dizzy with the speed of the royal magic. When her head stopped spinning, she saw Queen Titania holding out her wand and speaking the words of a spell.

"Crystal water, swirl and blend.
Show us Kirsty's dearest friend."

The pool rippled and a picture appeared before them. Kirsty saw Rachel sitting in a chair made of ice. A figure with spiky hair and a long cloak was

pacing around her.

"There's Jack Frost," said Ivy. "But where has he taken her?"

"That's not Jack Frost," said Kirsty. "That's Jilly Chilly, his sister. He was talking about her in the meadow, remember?"

"He must have taken Rachel to Jilly Chilly's home in the Ice Mountains," said the queen. "I can use my magic to send you there, but it will be up to you to save Rachel."

"We will," said Kirsty in a determined voice.

She reached for Ivy's hand. With a little nod, the queen waved her wand and the palace gardens vanished.

Chapter Fifteen
Meltdown

Kirsty and Ivy were standing outside
a tower made of ice. The arched door
was made of ice too, and someone had
roughly scratched words into it:

Jilly Chilly's Place. Go away!

"The last time I saw Jilly Chilly, I was
with Susie the Sister Fairy," said Kirsty.

"Susie used her magic to make Jilly Chilly and Jack Frost get along. I wonder if it's still working."

Ivy pushed on the door and it creaked open.

"There's only one way to find out," she whispered.

Inside there was nothing except a winding staircase carved from ice. The fairies fluttered upwards and heard voices.

"Now you have captured a silly fairy, we can make Queen Titania and King Oberon obey us," someone was saying.

"That's Jilly Chilly," Kirsty said.

"Yes," said Jack Frost's voice. "They will do anything to get one of their fairies back."

They cackled with laughter. Kirsty and Ivy reached the top of the stairs and found a doorway. Peeping around it, they saw Rachel sitting in a chair of ice. She had her head held high.

"You will never control Fairyland," Rachel said.

"Ha ha, she thinks someone's going to

rescue her," Jilly Chilly said in a mocking voice. "Foolish fairy. No one knows where you are."

"This is terrible," whispered Kirsty. "We can't reach Rachel without being seen."

She shivered, and Ivy raised her wand.

"Shall I magic up a coat to warm you up?" she asked.

Kirsty suddenly gripped Ivy's shoulders.

"That's it!" she said. "We just need to warm things up! Ivy, can you magic up enough heat to melt this tower?"

Her eyes sparkling, Ivy pressed the tip of her wand against the ice wall. A yellow-orange circle appeared and grew quickly, melting a hole in the wall. The warm glow spread across the wall, just like a flame licking at a piece of paper.

"What's happening?" cried Jilly Chilly in alarm. "My wall! My tower!"

"Run!" yelled Jack Frost.

He and Jilly Chilly zoomed down the melting staircase, as the tower disappeared around them. The wall in front of Kirsty and Ivy splashed to the ground, and they saw Rachel hovering in front of them.

"I knew you'd come!" she said, laughing.

She held out her hand to Ivy and gave

her the green serenity ball. Smiling, Kirsty
took the other ball from her pocket and
gave that to Ivy too. The Worry Fairy
smiled.

"Thank you from the bottom of my
heart," she said. "This is the perfect end to
our adventure."

Rachel looked down and saw Jilly

Chilly and Jack Frost below, shaking their fists.

"I think it's also the perfect moment to leave," she said, laughing.

"I'll send you back to Olive House," said Ivy, giving them each a hug. "Thanks to you, I can help people to

work through their worries again."

"We're really glad we could help," said Kirsty.

There was a sudden flurry of snow and fairy dust, and then the best friends were once more sitting on a squashy beanbag in the sitting room of Olive House. Christy had just stepped forward to speak.

"Let's hear from some of our younger visitors first," she said, smiling at Rachel and Kirsty. "How do you girls feel about your time here?"

Rachel and Kirsty squeezed each other's hand.

"I feel as if all my worries have melted away," said Rachel with a smile.

"And I feel happy to have made some new friends," Kirsty added. "It's been a totally magical weekend!"

The End

**Now it's time for Kirsty and
Rachel to help ...**

Teri the
Trampolining Fairy

Read on for a sneak peek ...

"There she is!" Rachel Walker cried in
excitement. "Kirsty! Kirsty!"

She jumped out of her dad's car,
waving to her best friend. Kirsty Tate
waved back.

"Isn't this brilliant?" said Kirsty,
running up to Rachel and hugging her.
"Now there's a leisure centre halfway
between our homes, we can go to the
same after-school club."

"I love sharing things with you," said
Rachel, winking at Kirsty.

Kirsty winked back. She knew that Rachel was talking about their most precious secret. Their friendship was truly magical, because it had grown stronger with each adventure they shared as friends of Fairyland.

The girls looked up at the sign hanging over the door.

"Cool Kids Leisure Centre," Rachel read aloud. "I can't wait to see inside and choose a club."

"How are we going to decide?" asked Kirsty.

"There are taster classes for each of the clubs," said Mr Tate. "When you've tried them all out, you can choose which one you like best."

"Go and have fun," said Mr Walker. "We're going to try out the new gym, so we'll see you later."

Rachel and Kirsty picked up their sports bags and hurried into the leisure centre. Inside, a young woman jogged over to meet them.

"Hi, I'm Lucy," she said. "Welcome to Ice Cool! Are you here for the after-school club taster sessions?"

The girls nodded.

Read Teri the Trampolining Fairy to find out what adventures are in store for Kirsty and Rachel!

RAINBOW magic

Calling all parents, carers and teachers!
The Rainbow Magic fairies are here to help
your child enter the magical world of reading.
Whatever reading stage they are at, there's
a Rainbow Magic book for everyone!
Here is Lydia the Reading Fairy's guide to
supporting your child's journey at all levels.

Starting Out

Our Rainbow Magic Beginner Readers are perfect for first-time readers who are just beginning to develop reading skills and confidence. Approved by teachers, they contain a full range of educational levelling, as well as lively full-colour illustrations.

①

Developing Readers

Rainbow Magic Early Readers contain longer stories and wider vocabulary for building stamina and growing confidence. These are adaptations of our most popular Rainbow Magic stories, specially developed for younger readers in conjunction with an Early Years reading consultant, with full-colour illustrations.

②

Going Solo

The Rainbow Magic chapter books – a mixture of series and one-off specials – contain accessible writing to encourage your child to venture into reading independently. These highly collectible and much-loved magical stories inspire a love of reading to last a lifetime.

③

www.rainbowmagicbooks.co.uk

"Rainbow Magic got my daughter reading chapter books. Great sparkly covers, cute fairies and traditional stories full of magic that she found impossible to put down" – Mother of Edie (6 years)

"Florence LOVES the Rainbow Magic books. She really enjoys reading now" – Mother of Florence (6 years)

The Rainbow Magic Reading Challenge

Well done, fairy friend – you have completed the book!
This book was worth 10 points.

See how far you have climbed on the
Reading Rainbow opposite.

The more books you read, the more points you will get,
and the closer you will be to becoming a Fairy Princess!

Do you want your own Reading Rainbow?
1. Cut out the coin below
2. Go to the Rainbow Magic website
3. Download and print out your poster
4. Add your coin and climb up the Reading Rainbow!

There's all this and lots more at
www.rainbowmagicbooks.co.uk

You'll find activities, competitions, stories, a special
newsletter and complete profiles of all the
Rainbow Magic fairies. Find a fairy with your name!